Buddie

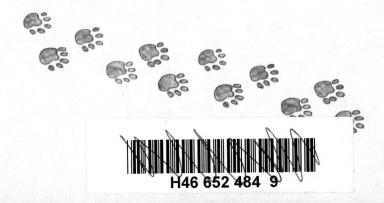

Buddie
The Trampolining Bear

Sarah Cooper
Illustrated by Linda Owen

BUMPKIN BOOKS

For the children in my life,
with beary much love,
S.C.

For my daughter, Alexandra,
who is also an arctophile
(someone who loves bears),
L.O.

First published in Great Britain in 2012
by Bumpkin Books, Oxfordshire

British Library Cataloguing in Publication Data:
a catalogue record for this book is available from the British Library

ISBN 978-0-9572086-1-2

www.trampoliningbear.com

Contents

1. Delivery Day

High in the mountains, surrounded by evergreen forests, lived a boy called Bouncer. With his nose pressed against the front window, he watched eagerly as a large lorry pulled up outside the log cabin.

"Mum! It's here. It's arrived!" shouted Bouncer, jumping up and down with delight.

The driver climbed out of the cab with some paperwork in his hand. As he walked up the path, Bouncer and his mum flung open the front door.

"Mrs Summer Sault? This delivery's for you. Sign here please," said the driver.

Summer signed quickly and hurried outside. Four strong men were carefully lowering massive boxes off the back of the lorry and onto the ground.

"Wow!" exclaimed Bouncer. "We've been waiting for this for months!"

Summer directed the men through the gates and into the back garden. "On the grass please," she called, "right in the middle, away from the trees."

The men unpacked the boxes and laid out all the pieces, like a gigantic jigsaw puzzle.

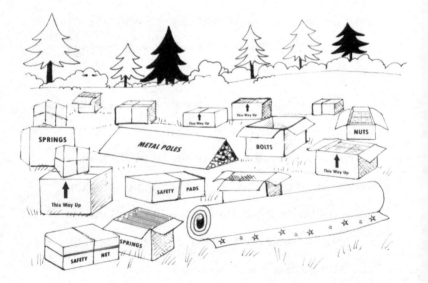

"It's the biggest trampoline in the world!" Bouncer told the men proudly. "My mum designed it herself. She won a gold medal for trampolining you know!"

"Now *that's* impressive!" said the driver.

Summer ruffled Bouncer's hair warmly, kissing his head with pride. "I did," she said, "but I've had this trampoline made especially for Bouncer. He's got *great* potential. He was a bouncy baby from the moment he was born." She smiled to herself, remembering how Bouncer had got his name. "As the doctors tried to weigh him on the hospital scales," she explained, "his legs wriggled, his arms stretched high in the air and he *bounced* up and down!"

"We'd better get building then," chuckled the driver, nodding to his team.

"I just can't wait to try it out!" yelled Bouncer, as he leapt around impatiently.

The men got to work straight away, following the longest list of instructions that they had ever seen. After two days, the trampoline was finally ready.

It was the size of a huge, rectangular swimming pool. The shimmering, sky blue mat was covered in twinkling silver stars. On top of the springs were thick, cushioned pads and the sparkling safety net around the trampoline was transparent.

As soon as the last bolt was securely in place on the colossal steel frame, Summer thanked the men and Bouncer slipped through the safety net and jumped onto the enormous, star-covered mat.

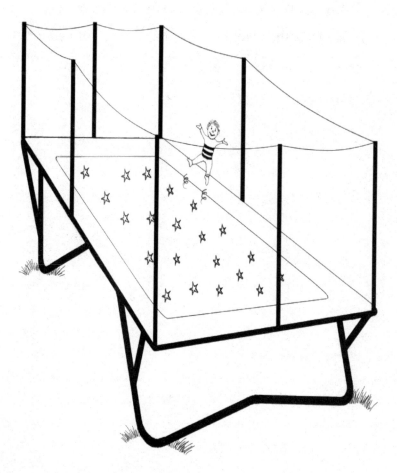

"Happy, bounciest me!" he squealed as he soared high into the air, his cheeks flushed with excitement. Waving goodbye to the men as they drove away, he yelled, "Look at me! I'm on top of the world!"

Bouncer's trampoline was his pride and joy. As he bounced, the twinkling stars on the mat seemed to spring into the air with him. It was a **very** special trampoline.

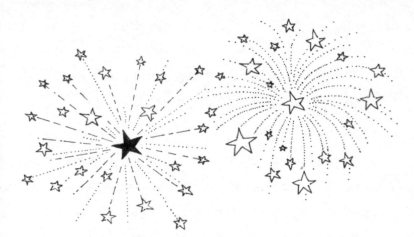

2. Paw Prints

If Bouncer had time before school, he would race down the garden and leap onto the trampoline. After warming up, he liked to practise his latest routines. Then, when he got home from school, he'd rush outside to work on his moves. Summer would sit on the veranda watching Bouncer. She was a trampoline coach, so she could help her son a lot.

Being outdoors on the trampoline, or taking part in competitions across the country, was when Bouncer felt happiest of all.

One morning, the same as any other, Bouncer hurried down the garden. As he pulled himself up onto the trampoline, he stopped. His eyes widened and his jaw dropped. Right before him, on the shimmering mat, were prints … paw prints … **bear** paw prints.

There was a neat muddy line of them leading from the edge of the mat to the centre, then hundreds of them in a mass in the middle, then another neat muddy line off the mat! Somebody had been bouncing on *his* trampoline!

Bouncer eyed
the bushes and
trees around
him carefully.
He heard a rustle
in the leaves but it
was just a chipmunk

scurrying about. Then a noise startled him above his
head, but it was only a couple of birds fluttering
through the branches. Bouncer had an uneasy feeling
in his tummy that someone was watching him...

Just then Summer called from the backdoor.
"Let's go Bouncer, let's go!" It was time for her to
take Bouncer to school. Hurrying him into the car,
she started the engine and switched on the radio,
singing along to the music at the top of her voice.

"Mum! Mum! There are paw prints on my
trampoline!" shouted Bouncer, trying to get
Summer's attention.

"Yes Love! Shhh now! Don't wind me up!" She
was too busy listening to her favourite programme.

Bouncer decided to text his dad instead. He lived overseas so they only got to see each other in the holidays but they spoke on the phone as much as they could. Taking his mobile out of his pocket he texted:

Text 08:15am
To   Dad

BEAR PAW PRINTS ON MY TRAMPOLINE DAD!

Two minutes later, Bouncer's phone beeped.

LUCKY THEY'RE NOT ELEPHANT PRINTS! his dad replied.

Bouncer sighed. *Parents!* he thought to himself. *They're impossible!*

When they pulled up in the school car park,
Bouncer tried again to get his mum to listen, but
Summer was deep in thought, going through a new
trampoline routine in her head.

"Later Bouncer, we'll talk about it later," she
said, kissing him on the head and hurrying him into
school. Then she headed off to the Sports Centre for
the day, to coach trampolining.

Bouncer took off his coat and walked into the classroom. He wanted to tell his teacher, Mrs Blossom, about the prints but she made all the children line up in silence, ready for assembly.

When it was sharing time and Bouncer was sat with his classmates, waiting to listen to each other's 'News', his hand shot up in the air. Finally, Mrs Blossom chose him to speak and he stood up in front of everyone. He thought he might burst with excitement.

"Well?" said Mrs Blossom. "What news would you like to share with us Bouncer?"

"This morning there were paw prints on my trampoline!" he blurted out.

"Paw prints?" exclaimed Mrs Blossom, "from your cat, Bouncer?"

"I don't have a cat," he replied, shaking his head.

"Well what kind of paw prints did you see Bouncer?" asked his teacher. "Were they small prints, maybe a squirrel or a racoon ran across your trampoline?"

"No … not a squirrel *or* a racoon Mrs Blossom. **They were … BEAR** prints!"

Bouncer's classmates started giggling and doing crazy bear actions, arms raised above their heads and mouths stretched wide, growling fiercely.

"Well Bouncer, that's certainly interesting news," said Mrs Blossom. "Maybe you have a bouncing bear in your garden?"

The class started laughing uncontrollably. Bouncer sat down in his seat feeling hurt and deflated. He *knew* what bear prints looked like and *there were* bear prints on his trampoline. The day dragged by slowly, with endless bear jokes and growls from his classmates. Even his best friend Ed joined in and pretended to be a bear, rubbing his back up and down on a doorframe, using it like a scratching post, as bears do! Bouncer was not amused.

WELCOME TO
MRS BLOSSOM'S
CLASS

As soon as he got home from school, he dropped his bag in the hallway and raced outside. Jumping up onto the trampoline, there, before him, were the paw prints he had seen that morning. Bouncer

Bouncer Sault

used the sleeves of his jumper to wipe the mat clean. There was just time to warm up and do three quick routines before tea.

As he got down from the trampoline he glanced at the trees and the bushes around him. For a split second, through the leaves, he thought he saw the glint of two sparkling eyes...

That night, when Bouncer climbed into bed, he wondered *who* might be climbing onto *his* trampoline! But he knew that it wouldn't be wise to go out exploring alone, as there really were wild bears in the forest where he lived.

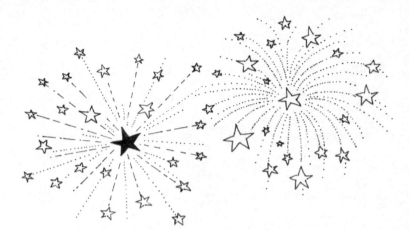

3. The Sleepover

At the weekend, Bouncer had Ed to stay for a sleepover. The boys spent the afternoon playing outside on the trampoline. Bouncer had a competition coming up so he wanted to show Ed his latest routine. As he finished his performance with a bow, Ed clapped and cheered at the top of his voice.

"That was amazing mate!"

"Thanks Ed," beamed Bouncer, catching his breath, "your turn now."

Ed clambered onto the trampoline and started to warm up. He had great fun doing tuck jumps, seat drops and an occasional star jump, but he was a computer whizz kid at heart. He much preferred bouncing computer ideas around in his head, to bouncing about on a trampoline!

After pizza for tea, the boys watched a movie with a big bag of popcorn to share. Then they brushed their teeth and put on their pyjamas. Ed loved staying over as Bouncer had bunk beds in his room and he let him sleep on the top. Lying on his tummy, his head resting on the pillow, Ed enjoyed a great view of the back garden from up there. With the window open a little, he liked to feel the cool night air breeze over him.

In the moonlight, Ed could see Bouncer's enormous trampoline, and the stars on the huge mat looked as if they were *really* twinkling.

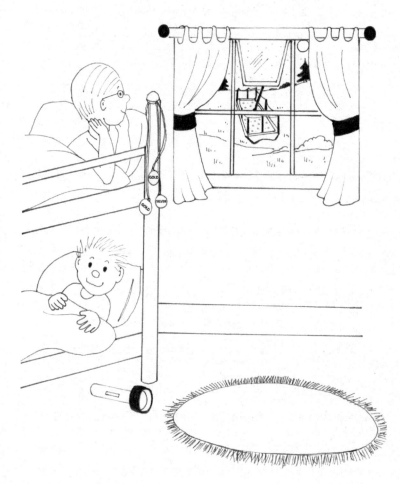

Once the boys were settled under their duvets, Summer came in to tuck them up snugly.

"Now NO midnight exploring please. NONE. You stay IN your beds. Are you listening to me? We know there are bears out in the forest, so stay safe inside. Boys?"

"Yes Mum, okay, we're listening," assured Bouncer.

"Yes Summer! Don't worry about us. We won't move a muscle," agreed Ed. "We *don't* want to come nose-to-nose with a bear!"

"We know your rules," added Bouncer, and together the boys recited them off by heart:

"<u>Number 1</u> - Don't go outdoors at night.
<u>Number 2</u> - Only go into the forest with an adult.
<u>Number 3</u> - Never leave food out to attract bears."

"Very impressive," laughed Summer as she kissed the boys goodnight. "Sleep tight then, don't let the big bears bite!" she joked, closing the bedroom door behind her. It'd been a very long week and she was exhausted. Crawling into bed, she switched off the light and fell asleep as soon as her head touched the pillow.

Back at the bunk beds, the boys were busy telling each other the scariest stories they could think of, giving themselves that tingly feeling that makes the hairs stand up on the back of your neck.

Just as they were drifting off to sleep, there was a rustling of bushes and a crunching of dried leaves on the forest floor outside the bedroom window. Then they heard something scurry across the grass, and stop. Both boys sat bolt upright.

Bouncer's eyes were wide open, his heart was pounding.

Ed turned as white as a sheet and got an uneasy feeling in his tummy.

All was quiet for a moment. Then, they heard a strange noise. It sounded like someone was … bouncing on the trampoline…

"What is *that*?" whispered Bouncer. "Something's out there! Have a look through the window Ed."

"I need my glasses mate, they're on the windowsill."

Bouncer felt around in the dark for his torch. He switched it on and shone it up at the window.

Spotting his glasses Ed put them on as quickly as he could. Very cautiously, he lifted his head over the edge of the pillow and looked outside.

"Get up here! Get up here QUICK!" he gasped. "You're not going to believe this!"

Bouncer leapt out of bed and flew up the ladder onto the top bunk. Lying alongside Ed they peeped out the open window and into the dark garden.

There, right there on the trampoline … in the cool, shimmering moonlight, was…

A BOUNCING BEAR!

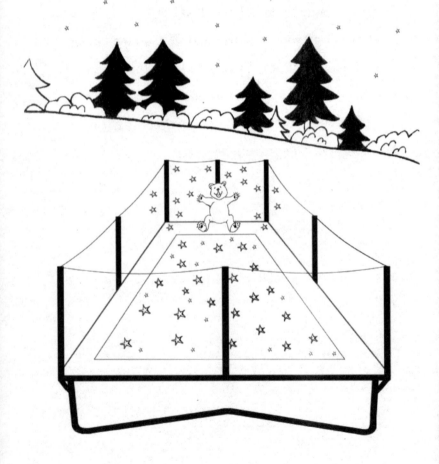

High into the air sprang the bear. It appeared to be doing some warm up moves. Then ... it did one of Bouncer's routines, perfectly from beginning to end! This bear was good, *really* good! The boys were speechless. As the bear bounced, they just gawped, their heads moving up and down, up and down, as they watched in amazement.

All of a sudden, the twinkling stars on the trampoline mat seemed to spring to life and danced up into the night air around the bear. They sparkled like glistening diamonds.

"Can you believe it?" murmured Ed. "We *must* be dreaming!"

"We're *not*!" said Bouncer, keeping his voice as quiet as he could. "It's real. *Really* real. Remember what I told the class Ed?"

"Oh yeah ... you weren't joking!"

"Err NO! I wasn't. There *were* bear paw prints on my trampoline! I *was* telling the truth!"

"You sure were mate! Sorry!" said Ed, nudging Bouncer on the arm. "I didn't believe you."

"Well you do now, right?"

"Err YES! I do … must be dreaming though." Ed rubbed his eyes, tweaked his hair and pinched himself to be a thousand per cent sure he was actually awake.

Once again, both boys peeked back out through the bedroom window. Sure enough, there before their eyes, as true and as real as ever, was **A BEAR!**

"Mrs Blossom was right Bouncer! You really do have a bouncing bear in your garden!" exclaimed Ed, and he burst out laughing.

"Shhh or you'll scare it away," muttered Bouncer crossly, putting his finger up to Ed's lips. "It looks like a cub."

Suddenly, the bear stopped bouncing. With its nose sniffing the air, it padded over to the side of the shimmering mat. Slipping between the safety nets, the bear held on to the edge of the trampoline. Then it swung by its paws, backwards and forwards, before dropping down onto the grass.

"Gulp!" went the boys, frozen with fear.

The bear padded towards the log cabin, its nose twitching and its eyes sparkling in the moonlight. The boys held their breath. With their noses poking over Ed's pillow, they watched from the safety of the top bunk. The bear got closer and closer.

As it walked across the grass, twinkling stars sprinkled from its paws and filled the air around it. Not daring to move a muscle, Bouncer and Ed stayed as still as they could. The bear walked right over to the log cabin, put its nose up in the air and inhaled deeply. Being curious, it wanted to see where the sound of laughter had come from. Standing on its back legs, the bear leant its big paws against the side of the log cabin and peered up at the bedroom window.

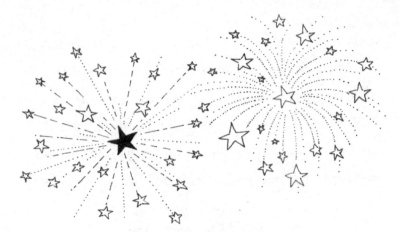

4. A Magical Night

Bouncer and Ed's hearts were hammering in their chests. They could hear the bear breathing just outside the open window. It was so close its breath steamed up the glass!

Ed opened his mouth to scream but Bouncer shook his head fiercely. "Nooo!" he urged Ed, under his breath. "St-st-stay quiet. This bear's different! It's m-m-magic! It's c-c-covered in twinkling stars!" Bouncer's voice was quavering, his heart was racing and his palms were sweating.

Too scared to watch what might happen next, Ed dived under his duvet.

Peeping out of the window, Bouncer could see the bear's beady eyes twinkling in the moonlight. He was sure its jaws would open and … they did!

"THANKS!" said the bear in a growly kind of way.

"F-f-for what?" stammered Bouncer.

"For letting me use your trampoline, Bouncer!" giggled the bear, fluttering its long eyelashes.

"Th-th-that's okay," Bouncer replied, stunned that the bear in his garden was not only a better trampolinist than he was, but spoke *and* knew his name! "H-h-how come you're so g-g-good?" he asked, "and how do you know my n-n-name?"

"I've been watching you and your mum for weeks on your trampoline. I've taught myself, and I've heard your mum calling you," explained the bear.

"Oh, I guess that makes sense," said Bouncer, relaxing slightly. "And w-w-what's your name?"

"Buddie!" replied the bear. "Bud for short. I'm a girl and I'm one and a half."

"Good to meet you Bud," Bouncer said, feeling a little calmer.

"You too," agreed the bear.

"Me three!" piped up Ed, as he crept out from under his duvet, feeling a tiny bit braver. "I'm Ed," he said, waving down at the bear through the open window.

"Hi Ed," beamed Buddie, baring the whitest set of the sharpest teeth. "It's GRRRRRRRrrrrrrreat to meet you."

Bouncer and Ed shot backwards in surprise, remembering *they were* face-to-face with a BEAR!

"I'm just kidding around!" chuckled Buddie, as she sat down on the grass in the moonlight. "My mum's back at our den. She'd be furious if she knew *I* was talking to *humans*. The rule is my brother and I have to stay as far away from *you* as possible," she explained, "but I love your trampoline so much I just can't resist it. Now us bears can be scary and we're certainly hairy, but I'm different. I'd like us to be friends, and if you don't mind, I'd *love* another go on your trampoline?"

"Absolutely!" grinned Bouncer.

"Will you come outside and watch?" Buddie asked. She smiled cheekily up at the boys and fluttered her eyelashes. She was a very pretty bear, with her beady eyes, rounded ears and thick coat, still covered in sparkling stars.

"We'll watch you from the veranda Bud, but we won't come any closer if that's okay?" suggested Bouncer. "We wouldn't want to upset your mum bear, if she came out of the forest looking for you."

"Good point!" nodded Ed. "You know how protective parents can be! My mum says we must 'TAKE CARE and be BEAR AWARE' at all times, *and* stay as far away from bears as we can."

"I'm one-of-a-kind," giggled Buddie. "How many bouncing bears do you know, who talk *and* have stars twinkling out of their paws?!"

Bouncer looked at Ed and Ed looked at Bouncer.

"And I'll keep my claws, my jaws and my strong bear paws to myself!" Bud promised.

Giving each other a nod, the boys crept down off the top bunk and put on their dressing gowns and slippers. Bouncer opened the door as quietly as he could and led the way. They stopped outside Summer's bedroom and listened. She was snoring soundly so they tiptoed into the lounge. Flicking on his torch, Bouncer steered them round the coffee table, past the sofa and out through the kitchen to the back door. Reaching up tall he slid back the top bolt and turned the key. Then Bouncer grabbed a can of bear spray from the shelf.

"I think we'll take this, just in case we need it," he said, slipping the can into his dressing gown pocket.

"Great idea mate!" agreed Ed. "Let's stay on the veranda and keep a safe distance between us and the bear!"

The boys snuck outside. They watched as Buddie swung herself onto the trampoline and started warming up again. As she sprung into the air, one move flowing effortlessly into the next, sparkling stars sprinkled from her paws.

With their mouths wide open and their eyes twinkling, they watched in awe. Buddie bounced higher, straighter and faster than Bouncer could. After running through three of his routines from beginning to end, she stopped and did a cheeky little curtsey. The boys clapped softly and cheered quietly, as they didn't want to wake Summer up.

Buddie climbed down off the trampoline and headed back across the grass towards the log cabin. She stopped a sensible distance away, so as not to frighten the boys. Sitting down on the grass, she grinned cheekily up at them on the veranda. Stars sprinkled from the pads of her paws on to the ground and sparkled all around her.

"You're grrrreat!" laughed Bouncer.

"Bearrrrilliant!" tittered Ed.

"I've learnt it all from you Bouncer, and your mum," Buddie said. "She's a great coach isn't she?"

"She sure is Bud. She's the best."

Ed was staring at the twinkling stars as they floated into the air around Buddie. "Where do your

stars come from Bud?" he asked, mesmerised by
them.

"I don't know," she replied, studying her front
paws carefully, as tiny stars continued to fizz into the
air. "When I had my first go on your trampoline it
was a moonlit night. The Great Bear constellation
was so bright." Buddie pointed up into the dark sky
above them. "Look!" she said to the boys. "That
group of stars right there. *That's* the Great Bear
constellation."

Bouncer and Ed followed Buddie's paw and saw
the shape of a starry bear glimmering overhead.

"I remember the sky was full of shooting stars too," she explained. "It felt like the Great Bear was watching me and smiling, as if he was real. Then your trampoline mat seemed to spring to life and the stars started dancing around me. Ever since then, whenever I bounce my paws tingle with energy and all this sparkling stardust sprinkles into the air."

"Wow *that is* magic!" exclaimed Bouncer, his eyes wide.

"Beary magic!" whispered Ed.

"I guess so," Buddie replied, as she got up onto all fours, stretched her limbs slowly and wiggled her small tail. "It's time for my bed now," she said, standing on her back legs. Then Buddie crossed her paws in front of her like a big kiss and blew one each to the boys. They watched in astonishment as stars formed into a kiss shape in the air and twinkled towards them, covering them in glittering stardust. The tips of Bouncer's spiky hair and the rims of Ed's glasses glimmered.

"Check out your hair mate!" giggled Ed.

"Take a look at your glasses!" laughed Bouncer.

"Stellar!" gasped Ed, holding his glasses out in front of him.

Promising to see each other again soon, Bouncer and Ed waved goodbye to Buddie as she padded back to her den in the forest.

The boys tiptoed wearily into the log cabin and locked the back door. They crept back to Bouncer's bedroom and climbed into bed. In the darkness, the tiniest stars fizzed and twinkled around them. They slept soundly for a good few hours, dreaming of bouncing bears and sparkling paws.

5. Porridge

As the dawn became day, sunlight streamed into the log cabin and the warm rays woke Summer from her dreams. She got out of bed, put on her dressing gown and headed through to the kitchen to make some porridge for the boys' breakfast.

What a beautiful day, she thought to herself, opening the window and the back door.

The smell of freshly cooked oats in warm milk wafted up into the air and outside into the sunny morning.

"Wakey, wakey, sleepy heads!" Summer called as she pushed Bouncer's bedroom door open. "Breakfast's ready!"

The boys peered at her through the sleepiest eyes.

"You look like you've been up most of the night!" she exclaimed.

"We have," Bouncer croaked. "We met a bouncing bear."

"Yeah, we did," mumbled Ed drowsily.

"Don't wind me up boys. Now come and eat your porridge. It'll give you plenty of energy for your day." Summer went back to the kitchen and drizzled the sweetest, stickiest honey into the centre of the hot oats. "It's on the table," she called, as she headed off to take a shower and get dressed.

After their busy night, Bouncer and Ed's eyelids were too heavy to open and they drifted quickly back to sleep.

Now, as you can imagine, the smell of freshly cooked porridge and melting honey had reached the nostrils of a hungry little bear. Not being able to resist, Buddie's nose led her sleepily out of her den and through the forest to the log cabin.

Peeping in at the kitchen window she saw not one, but two very generous bowls of *heaven*! Licking her lips she snuck in at the back door and picked up the first bowl. Buddie poured it cheekily into her open mouth. In an instant it was all gone.

She rubbed her tummy contentedly. The warmth from the porridge spread through her, from the tips of her ears to the pads of her paws.

Buddie eyed the second bowl. *Now it would be greedy if I ate that too,* she pondered to herself, *but my tummy is still a bit rumbly and I'm sure Bouncer and Ed won't mind?*

Tiptoeing over to the bedroom door, Buddie took a sneaky peek inside. Both boys were snoring soundly, so she climbed onto a chair and picked up a spoon. She relished every single mouthful, especially the honey which she didn't mix in, but saved until last. It was her best bit. Feeling quite greedy but warm and fuzzy too, she licked her lips and wiped her mouth with the back of her furry paws. Then she waddled out the door and into the forest, ready for her morning snooze.

Back at the bunk beds, Bouncer and Ed finally stirred. Feeling hungry, they climbed out of bed and wandered into the kitchen. Eyeing the two bowls that were waiting for them on the table, they sat down dozily. Suddenly, their eyes widened and their jaws dropped.

"Someone's been eating our porridge," mumbled Bouncer.

"And they've eaten it all up," grumbled Ed.

Looking at each other they burst out laughing.

"What a *beary*, cheeky bear!" said Bouncer.

"What a beary, cheeky, *hungry* bear!" sniggered Ed.

"I'd far rather she ate our porridge, and not us," added Bouncer, remembering the moment they'd come face-to-face with the bear. Carefully rubbing the muddy paw prints from the sides of the bowls he called to Summer. "Can we have some more please Mum? We're still hungry."

"My! What a busy night you must have had," laughed Summer, as she came back into the kitchen.

"We really did meet a bear!" said Bouncer.

"Well I hope he was friendly!" giggled Summer, as she heated the milk and stirred in some oats.

"*He* was a *she*!" corrected Ed.

"Oh, he was a she, was she? Well I hope *she* was friendly?"

"She was, and she's much better at trampolining than me," explained Bouncer.

"Not possible," said Summer, as she poured more hot porridge into the bowls, topping it with the stickiest honey. "No one is better than my bouncing boy. A bear on the trampoline! Honestly! Whatever next?" and she ruffled her son's hair warmly, kissing his head with pride. "The International Trampolining Event is next month. We'd better get some more practice in hadn't we?" she suggested.

Bouncer nodded keenly.

"Can I come to the stadium and watch please?" asked Ed, looking at Summer hopefully.

"Of course you can. Bouncer loves having you there. You're a great friend Ed," she replied.

Summer walked over to the table and put down the bowls of porridge for the boys. Picking up their spoons eagerly they thanked her. As they tucked into their breakfast for the first time, Buddie slept off two breakfasts in her den in the forest nearby.

6. Mission B.I.T.E.

The weeks flew past and day after day Bouncer practised his trampolining routine for the upcoming competition. He was in the under twelves category. Even though Bouncer was only ten, he had sailed through the local and regional rounds. He was one of the best young trampolinists in the country. His bedroom was filled with an incredible collection of all the medals and trophies that he'd won.

Before and after school Bouncer trained. Summer stood by the trampoline, calling out instructions and helping him to perfect his routine. While Bouncer worked through his moves, Buddie hid quietly behind the bushes and trees, watching and memorising everything he did.

As Summer helped Bouncer with his fitness - jogging around the garden together, skipping, doing press ups and sit ups - little did she know that a very special bear was doing the same in the forest nearby.

While Bouncer drank lots of water, milk and juice, and ate the healthiest foods – fruit, vegetables, protein and pasta - to keep his energy up and his body in top shape, the little bear ate and drank plenty too. Buddie filled her tummy with grasses, berries, leaves and cherries, plus a lot of ants, beetles, wasps, bees, grubs and her favourite of all - honey. After exercising she'd walk through the forest to have a long, refreshing drink from the stream, and cool herself down.

On clear nights, when the stars were bright in the sky, Buddie practised on the trampoline. The Great Bear constellation looked down on her from above and smiled. Bouncer watched Buddie from his bedroom window, and she always stopped by to say hello to him. As the nights passed by, the boy and the bear became very good friends.

"You're an amazing trampolinist Bud," he said one night. "You *really are* one-of-a-kind. I wish you could take part in the International Trampolining Event too you know? You so deserve to win a medal after all your hard work."

Buddie grinned. "I think you're forgetting I'm a bear!" she said.

"You're my friend," replied Bouncer, "and you're good, extremely good."

"Well," said Buddie, scratching behind her ear thoughtfully. "If you can get me there, I'll give it my best shot!"

"Leave it with me!" said Bouncer excitedly.

As they said goodnight to each other, Bouncer gave Buddie a wink out of the window. Then his mind sprang into action. He bounced idea after idea around in his brain.

Now Bouncer knew only too well that he'd tried to tell his mum *and* his dad about Buddie and how good she was, but they had just scolded him. "A bouncing bear! How ridiculous! Now *don't* tell fibs, *don't* wind me up please and *no* more stories! What an over-active imagination!" they'd said.

Mrs Blossom had laughed, and Bouncer's classmates had made fun of him, so he'd kept very quiet about Buddie at school.

If his parents, his teacher *and* his classmates wouldn't believe him, Bouncer knew *he* had to come up with a plan.

It took a few days and lots of ideas, but Bouncer's hard work had paid off:

Mission B.I.T.E. was underway.

Bear's International Trampolining Event, giggled Bouncer to himself.

Ed was his accomplice and between them, Buddie *would* be at the International Trampolining Event.

The day of the competition arrived and Summer, Bouncer and Ed set off for the stadium. Summer was filled with excitement. She was totally unaware that in Ed's large, brown bag, in the boot of her car, was a bouncing bear!

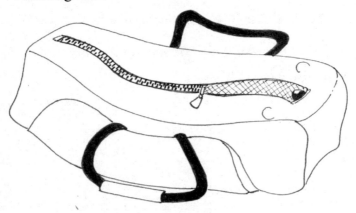

Bouncer was so grateful he had Ed and together they hoped Mission B.I.T.E. would succeed.

Now, let's get back to the boot of Summer's car! There was Buddie, tucked up carefully in Ed's bag. It was unzipped a little so there was a perfect nose-sized hole for her to breathe out of. She had plenty of snacks to eat and a bottle of lemonade to drink on the journey.

Luckily for the boys, Summer was singing along loudly to her favourite radio program. This helped to drown out the loud crunching, munching, scrunching and smacking of lips coming from the boot, not to mention the enormous burps, hiccups *and* pongy bear smells caused by Buddie guzzling her fizzy lemonade far too quickly!

After a while, Summer started to get a bit fed up of the noises – *and the whiffs*, wafting over from the back of the car.

"My you're eating noisily boys! Don't slurp your drinks now, it's rude. Stop burping in my ear. What a stink! Do remember your manners," and so she carried on.

"Sorry Mum!" "Sorry Summer!" "We'll try to keep the noise down!" exclaimed the boys.

Bouncer leant over the back seat into the boot to give Buddie a gentle prod.

"GRRRRrrrrrrrrrrrrrrrrrrrrr!" replied the bag stroppily.

"GRRRRRRRRRRRRRRRRRRRR!"

"*Enough* with the bear noises boys," shouted Summer. "Bouncer! *Will* you sit down? What are you doing stretching into the boot?" She was trying to concentrate on her driving but had to keep a close eye on what the boys were up to in her rear-view mirror. She was beginning to lose her cool and become ratty.

Bouncer was getting pinker and hotter and Ed was trying in vain to keep the peace in the car.

Finally Buddie had eaten enough and her tummy was full. She closed her eyes wearily and dozed off to sleep, snoring so loudly that the back seat vibrated. Ed, beginning to panic, pretended to fall asleep too, and snored like a very large bear! It was certainly a challenge but Mission B.I.T.E. was coming together.

At the stadium Summer parked the car. Bouncer and Ed insisted on carefully lifting the large, brown bag out of the boot, lowering it gently to the ground.

The boys carried a handle each.

"Whatever have you got in there?" Summer asked. "Sure looks very heavy."

"It's BEARY heavy!" answered Ed, tittering to himself.

Bouncer grinned at him and both boys noticed Buddie's shiny black nose twitching crossly! She'd had enough of being in a bag. She needed to brush her fur, stretch her paws and smooth her claws ready for her routine. Thankfully, Summer was distracted, looking for her ticket in her bag and checking the boys had their passes for the arena.

7. The Stadium

Once inside the stadium the International Trampolining Event got underway. Ed stayed with Bouncer to give him support. Summer found her seat and waved down to the boys in the arena. Butterflies were dancing in her tummy with anticipation. She hoped Bouncer would do his best and not be too nervous in front of such a vast audience.

On Bouncer's team there were ten children, six boys and four girls. They were competing against the best young trampolinists from places all over the world. Everyone was so busy warming up, stretching, waving to their families and getting last minute tips from their coaches, that they didn't notice Ed hide his bag behind a row of chairs. He unzipped it carefully and helped out a very excited little bear. While Buddie brushed her fur, stretched her limbs, pointed her paws and smoothed her claws with her claw file, Ed had a job to do.

Claw file

Bear hair brush

The timing was crucial. Seeing that the judges had not yet taken their seats, Ed glanced over at Bouncer and gave him a quick nod. Walking calmly up the steps to the judges' area and their panel of computers, he slipped into the middle chair. His fingers sprang into action and clicked speedily over the keyboard as he entered the final contestant's details:

Name: BUDDIE   Age: 1 year   Female BEAR!

Then he removed a memory stick from his pocket and inserted it into the computer. A few more clicks and Buddie's music for her routine was loading on to the system. Waiting as patiently as he could, Ed watched the seconds clicking down on the screen in front of him. Done. He put the stick back into his pocket. The job was complete.

As coolly as he could, not wanting to draw attention to himself, he swung his legs off the chair and hurried back down the steps. Just as he reached the bottom, the 'PRIVATE' door swung open and the judges marched out into the stadium, looking as fierce and focused as ever.

"Job's done mate. Mission B.I.T.E.'s on track. Buddie's up last," said Ed quietly, as he patted Bouncer on the back.

The competition was in full swing. As Ed sat watching the trampolinists, Buddie peeped over his shoulder. She was very careful not to be spotted. At last it was Bouncer's turn. Just as he finished his warm up stretches, he heard the booming voice of the announcer over the loudspeaker:

"BOUNCER SAULT ON THE TRAMPOLINE. PLEASE TAKE YOUR STARTING POSITION."

The crowd applauded and Summer rose to her feet, clapping loudly and cheering for Bouncer at the top of her voice.

"GO BOUNCER! GO BOUNCER!" roared his team, knowing he was their best chance of a gold medal.

Bouncer took deep breaths, trying to calm his rapid heartbeat and fill his lungs with oxygen. Ed watched proudly as his best mate performed a brilliant routine, and from behind his shoulder, peeked a nervous little bear!

Bouncer stood in the centre of the trampoline, bowed to the judges and waved to the roaring crowds. His scores clicked up on the board overhead:

9.5	9	10	9	10	9.5	10	9

"Bouncer Sault has done it again," praised the announcer. "Another outstanding performance with tremendous height throughout the routine and an average score of **9.5**. Surely that's put him in top position for the gold medal? An excellent routine."

Bouncer dismounted from the trampoline. Flushed with pride and adrenalin, he waved at Summer and gave her a thumbs up. Then he walked swiftly back to Ed, who was waiting patiently on the chairs. Sitting down to put on his tracksuit top, Bouncer felt a warm lick on his neck.

"Well done Bouncer," said Buddie. "That was truly grrreat!"

"Thanks Bud," he whispered, reaching behind the seat to give his friend a good luck scratch behind her ears. She loved that.

"My turn soon!" she said excitedly.

At that moment, a quiet hush crept over the stadium.

Everyone's attention turned to the judging panel. The judges were squabbling, shaking their heads and waggling their fingers at each other. Papers were flying and voices were raised. Their words all jumbled into a frenzy of heated discussion.

Is she *really* a **BEAR**? Never heard of such a competitor!

Who's entered her? 1 year old! She's just a baby!

We can**NOT** have **bears** at the Internationals! Whatever next?

Who's loaded her music onto the system? What is this? **A ZOO**?

The judges' faces were becoming redder and shinier as they continued to fret and started to sweat. It was not a pretty sight. The audience was getting restless and twitchy. They wanted to know what all the fuss was about. Before long they started clapping impatiently, slowly but LOUDLY!

"ENOUGH!" bellowed the head judge. "It is *not* for us to say YES or to say NO to this competitor. Everyone must get a fair chance to take part today. And if we need to be fair, then let's give Buddie BEAR her turn!"

Over the loudspeaker came the booming voice of the announcer:

"BUDDIE BEAR ON THE TRAMPOLINE. PLEASE TAKE YOUR STARTING POSITION."

The clapping eased off.

"BUDDIE BEAR ON THE TRAMPOLINE, WILL YOU PLEASE TAKE YOUR STARTING POSITION? OUR LAST TRAMPOLINIST OF THE DAY IS BUDDIE BEAR! QUIET PLEASE. LADIES AND GENTLEMEN, QUIET PLEASE!"

From behind Bouncer, Ed and the row of chairs stepped Buddie, her head held high, her fur brushed and her claws smoothed. The audience could *not* believe their eyes.

"A bouncing bear!" gasped Summer. The butterflies in her tummy felt as if they were fluttering around wildly. *Whatever are those boys up to now?* she thought anxiously.

Walking as tall as she could, Buddie fluttered her eyelashes cutely at the boys and made her way to the trampoline. She sprung up onto the mat, did a cheeky little curtsey to the dumbstruck judges, then a gleeful wave to the awaiting spectators. She nodded to show she was ready to start and her music began.

What a routine it was! One effortless move led into another. Buddie enjoyed every single moment. Her love of trampolining shone out through her enormous bear smile.

Shocked to see a bear taking part in the competition, the audience sat in stunned silence. As Buddie's performance continued, however, they rose to their feet and started dancing in their seats, singing along and clapping eagerly to the beat of the music.

On the judging panel no one moved. They were speechless. As their jaws dropped and almost rested on their keyboards, Bouncer and Ed watched in amusement.

And to complete her routine, Buddie performed a grand finale where her paws showered sparkling stars up into the air like fireworks.

The music came to an end as she descended to the mat, surrounded by a flurry of starry glitter. Buddie finished with a full curtsey and applause erupted throughout the stadium.

She raised her head and waved proudly to Bouncer and Ed. Then she blew bear kisses to the spectators and threw twinkling stardust into the crowds with her paws. She felt, quite simply, on top of the world.

The judges, shaking their heads in disbelief, were unanimous:

10	10	10	10	10	10	10	10

Buddie *had* won first place.

8. Medals

As Buddie stood on the podium, the head judge shook her paw and kissed her furry cheeks rather gingerly. Tiny stars continued to fizz up into the air around the bouncing bear.

The judge hung the sparkling gold medal around Buddie's neck and presented her with a massive bouquet of flowers. Forgetting herself for a moment, she buried her face in the petals and stuck her tongue sneakily into one of the blooms, licking the tasty nectar.

"Delicious," she whispered to herself. "I'll save these for later!"

Standing proudly next to Buddie on the podium, in second place, was Bouncer. The judge gave him his well-deserved silver medal. Then in third place, receiving a bronze medal was Harry Spring Yee, the previous world trampolining champion.

Ed and Summer clapped so hard that their palms stung. Summer made her way down through the crowds to her son and wrapped her arms tightly around him. Standing close by with a beaming smile, a gold medal around her furry neck, her flowers, and an outstretched paw was the winning bear.

"Mrs Sault!" said Buddie. "I'm very happy to meet you."

"Call me Summer," she laughed, as she squeezed Buddie close to her. "That was out of this world!"

"Thank you," beamed Buddie. "You and Bouncer have taught me everything I know and I just *love* your trampoline."

The penny finally dropped. Summer chuckled. *Bouncer was telling me the truth*, she thought to herself, smiling warmly at Buddie.

"Well, you can use our trampoline as much as you wish little bear, and … I guess you'd like a lift home?"

"That would be great – but do I have to go in the boot?" asked Buddie.

"No, you must sit next to me in the passenger seat," insisted Summer. "Pride of place for the beary best bouncing bear in the world!"

"That'd be a first," said Buddie. "I've never *sat* in a car before!"

As you can imagine, there was huge media interest in the trampolining bear. A large room filled quickly with eager reporters, frantically snapping their cameras, filming, and asking Buddie an endless stream of questions:

After half an hour, Buddie raised her paw. "Shhh please," she requested. "That's quite enough for now. My ride home is waiting for me. I was smuggled here in the boot of a car but I'm very excited to announce that I'll be travelling home in the passenger seat!"

Beaming her best bear smile, being careful not to bare too many of her sharp teeth, Buddie took her final curtsey of the day.

Summer led the way through the crowd, and outside into the bright sunshine. She carried Buddie's flowers, while Bouncer and Ed held a bear paw each.

The boys clambered into the back of the car as Buddie jumped up proudly onto the passenger seat.

Summer strapped her in safely and they waved goodbye to everyone. Then they headed home, laughing, chattering and singing at the tops of their voices.

"Mission B.I.T.E.'s complete!" said Bouncer, giving Ed a hug, as they dropped him off at his house. "I couldn't have done it without you. You're the BEARst!"

"Yes! You're BEARilliant!" shouted Buddie, blowing kisses to Ed out of the car window. "Truly BEARilliant!"

Ed grinned, slung the empty bag over his shoulder and walked up the path to his front door, waving proudly to his friends.

As Summer pulled up outside their log cabin,
Buddie and Bouncer jumped out of the car, their
medals still swinging around their necks.

"Time for tea and toast," called Summer.

"With honey?" asked Buddie hopefully.

"*Of course*, with honey!" she laughed.

And there, round the kitchen table, sat Summer,
her bouncing boy and a very special bear, all
crunching, munching, scrunching and licking their
lips, as the warm toast melted the stickiest honey.

"I've had a wonderful day," said Buddie, wiping her mouth with the back of a furry paw. She wrapped her arms around Bouncer and Summer, giving them tender bear hugs. "Thank you from the tips of my ears to the pads of my paws!" she said.

Summer kissed the bear gently on her head and stroked her fur. Bouncer gave her a quick scratch behind her ears. She loved that. Then Buddie headed off down the garden with her gold medal, her tasty flowers and a spring in her step. At the edge of the forest she turned and waved a very happy paw to her friends.

"Enough bouncing for you for one day!" said Summer that night, as she tucked her son up tightly in bed.

"Until tomorrow," replied Bouncer sleepily, as his legs wriggled with excitement.

Now, as this story comes to an end, just remember one thing. If *you* ever climb onto a trampoline, look out for muddy paw prints – and maybe, somewhere in the bushes, you'll see the glint of two sparkling eyes.

To find out more about Bouncing Buddie Bear,

and have some fun, go to

www.trampoliningbear.com

 Design your very own trampoline mat.

 Colouring pages to print out and enjoy.

 Beary lovely things to make and do.

Sarah Cooper - Author

Sarah lives in Hertfordshire with her husband James, dog Bertie and a lot of teddy bears. They have more than twenty Godchildren, nieces and nephews. Sarah is a teacher and loves being surrounded by little people in the classroom and at home – playing, cooking, doing art and crafts, or going to the cinema, park, fair, zoo...

Most of all Sarah loves to write and share her stories with the children in her life, or listen to them reading to her. She first got the idea for Buddie when she was eleven, writing a story for her English teacher. Sarah's nickname is Sare-Bear!

Linda Owen - Illustrator

Linda also lives in Hertfordshire with her daughter and Raffi the dog, along with an odd assortment of bears. The oldest bear she has is over 100 years old and is called Olympia. Linda found her in an antique shop in Canada and put her on a flight back to London. Olympia is a very large bear indeed. She stands on all fours, on wheels, and children used to ride around on her.

Linda draws and paints most days and has just illustrated a children's book on historical costumes. It starts with a Roman soldier and ends with a modern girl.